This edition published by Parragon Books Ltd in 2014 and distributed by

Parragon Inc.
440 Park Avenue South, 13th Floor
New York, NY 10016
www.parragon.com

ISBN 978-1-4723-6727-3

Printed in China

Treasure Island

Based on the original story by
Robert Louis Stevenson

Illustrated by Steve Horrocks

Ye Olde Inn

PaRragon

Bath • New York • Cologne • Melbourne • Delhi
Hong Kong • Shenzhen • Singapore • Amsterdam

Squire Trelawney and Dr. Livesey have asked me to write down all the details about Treasure Island, from beginning to end, keeping nothing back but the whereabouts of the island, and that only because there may still be treasure to be found. I take up my pen and go back to the time when my parents kept the Admiral Benbow inn and the old seaman with the saber cut across his cheek first took up his lodging under our roof.

I remember him as if it were yesterday, glancing about suspiciously and whistling to himself, and then breaking out in that old sea song that he sang so often: "Fifteen men on the dead man's chest, yo-ho-ho, and a bottle of rum!"

"Much company here, mate?" he growled at my father, as he plodded up to our door, dragging a large chest behind him. My father shook his head.

"Then this is the place for me," he snarled. "Name's Billy Bones, but you can call me Captain."

He beckoned to me with his dirty, scarred hands. "Boy, if you keep an eye open for a seafaring man with one leg, I'll pay you a silver penny the first of every month."

I loved a mystery and promised him I would do his bidding.

The strange seaman stayed for months, but he never paid my parents a penny for his keep. Every day he strolled along the cove cliffs, looking out to sea with a telescope; every evening, he sat in the parlor drinking rum.

It was during the Captain's stay that my father became ill and passed away. Two mysterious events also occurred around this sad time, which rid us of the Captain.

The first happened one frosty morning, when the Captain was out on his usual cliff walk. A pale man, missing two fingers on his left hand and carrying a cutlass, came into the inn, sat down, and demanded a drink.

As he was asking me whether we had a captain staying with us, Billy Bones strode through the door.

"Hello, Bill," said the man. "You remember your ol' shipmate?"

The Captain gave a sort of gasp. "Black Dog!" he cried.

"And who else?" cackled the man.

"What do yer want?" whispered the Captain.

"I've come for what you've hidden in your sea chest," sneered Black Dog. "Hand it over, and there'll be no trouble."

"Never!" roared the Captain, and he pulled out his own cutlass.

There followed a terrible sword fight and then a cry of pain, and in the next instant, I saw Black Dog fleeing from the inn with blood streaming from his shoulder.

The Captain's face had turned a horrible color. "I've got to get away from here. Jim, help me. Black Dog and me sailed with a pirate named Captain Flint. I was his first mate, and he gave me for safekeeping a map of where he buried his treasure. The rest of his crew will be after me now, for sure." And with these words he reeled a little, caught himself with one hand against the wall, and then fell with a heavy thud to the floor.

According to our good friend Dr. Livesey, he'd had a stroke. Whether it was from too much rum or from shock, I'll never know.

While the Captain was recovering in bed, the second mysterious event occurred. I was outside the inn when I heard an odd tapping noise. I turned to see an old blind man trudging up the road toward me.

"Can any kind friend tell me where I am?" he cried.

"You are at the Admiral Benbow inn," I called out.

Suddenly, the man grabbed my arm and hissed in a cruel, cold voice, "Take me in to the Captain."

Terrified, I obeyed him. The sickly Captain paled even more when he saw the old man.

"Hold out your hand, Bill," growled the blind man, and he pressed a small piece of paper into the Captain's hand. He turned and, tapping his stick, left as suddenly as he had appeared.

Bill read the note on the back. "The Black Spot! The pirates, they're coming for me at ten o'clock tonight!" he gasped, as he leapt out of bed. In the next moment, with a peculiar sound, he fell to the floor. To my horror and great distress, he was dead.

With the Captain's last words weighing heavy on my heart, I ran to my mother and lost no time in telling her all that I knew, and perhaps should have told her long before. We realized we were now in a difficult and dangerous position. With little time to lose, we made our plans. We would have to leave the inn before the pirates arrived. We decided we would seek shelter and help from Dr. Livesey.

Before we left, my mother told me to search the Captain's dead body for the key to his sea chest. She was convinced there would be money in the chest, and some of the Captain's money—if indeed there was any—was certainly due to us for his stay at the inn. She said we should take what was owed to us, because it was not likely that our Captain's old shipmates, who would certainly be here before long, would be inclined to give up their booty in payment of the dead man's debts.

Overcoming my disgust at having to touch the dead Captain, I tore open his shirt at the neck, and there, hanging on a bit of dirty string, I found the key. We ran to the chest and unlocked it.

A strong smell of tobacco and tar rose from the interior. Underneath some clothes and an odd assortment of trinkets and shells, we found a bundle of papers tied up in oilcloth and a bag filled with coins from many countries. We grabbed the papers and some of the coins and crept out into the foggy night not a moment too soon. The sound of running footsteps came to our ears and, as we looked back, we could see the light of a lantern bobbing in the dark, heading toward our inn.

"My dear," said my mother suddenly, "take the money and run on. I am going to faint." And she crumpled to the ground.

I looked around in a panic. By good fortune, we were by a small bridge.
I managed to drag my mother a little way under the arch just as seven or
eight pirates, led by the old blind man, stormed the inn.

I could hear the fury in the blind man's voice as he cried, "Is Flint's map there?"

"The money's here, but I don't see no map," replied one of the men.

"It's that boy and his mother. They must have it! Scatter, lads, and find 'em."

I lay by the bridge and watched in horror as the pirates tore apart the inn in their desperate search. Suddenly, a sharp whistle pierced the night.

"We'll have to budge, mates. There's trouble on the way!" cried one of the men.

"You've got to find the map," screamed the blind man. "We'll be as rich as kings if you find it!"

But the other pirates, fearing for their own safety, grabbed the money and started running in all directions as the sound of galloping hooves came thundering down the road.

Screaming and cursing, the blind man staggered along the road, tapping his stick in a frenzy and, before I knew it, he had stumbled into the path of the galloping horses. The riders couldn't stop in time and, to my horror, the blind man was trampled to death under the hooves.

I leaped to my feet and hailed the riders. They were revenue officers who had heard some news about the pirates' intended raid and had been on their way to stop them. I hurriedly told them my story and about my fear that the pirates would be back for the bundle of papers I had taken from the Captain's chest.

After helping my mother to the village to recover from her faint, the supervising officer agreed to take me to see Dr. Livesey to give him the papers for safekeeping.

Dr. Livesey was dining with the squire, Mr. Trelawney, when I arrived.

The two men listened to my story with surprise and interest.

"You've heard of this Flint, I suppose?" said the doctor to the squire.

"Heard of him?" cried the squire. "He was the most bloodthirsty buccaneer that ever sailed!"

The doctor carefully opened the seals on one of the papers, revealing a map of an island, with three red crosses marked on it. By the last cross, written in a small neat hand, were the words: "Bulk of treasure here."

The squire picked up the map, his hands shaking with excitement.

There were more scribbles on the back of it. I didn't understand the meaning of these words, but they filled the squire and Dr. Livesey with delight.

"Livesey," said the squire, "we shall find this treasure! Tomorrow I will go to the port at Bristol, and in three weeks' time, I'll have the best ship, sir, and the choicest crew in England."

He turned to me. "Jim Hawkins, you'll make a famous cabin boy. You, Livesey, will be ship's doctor, and I'm admiral. We'll take some men with us that I know and trust, and we'll recruit the rest of the crew."

"All right," said the excited doctor. "I'll sail with you. But none of us must breathe a word about this map."

The weeks passed slowly, for I was eager to start our treasure hunt. Finally, one fine day, Dr. Livesey and I received a letter from Mr. Trelawney requesting that we join him in Bristol, ready for our adventure to Treasure Island. We would be sailing on the *Hispaniola*, the ship he had bought and fitted out. He had also gotten a crew together, complete with ship's cook, mate, and captain.

"Dear Livesey," he wrote. "By a stroke of good fortune, I fell in talk with an old sailor who wanted a good berth as a ship's cook. Long John Silver he is called, and he has lost a leg. Out of pure pity for his state of health, I employed him on the spot. He keeps a public house here and knows all the seafaring men in Bristol. Between Silver and myself, we have gotten together a crew of the toughest old salts imaginable—not pretty to look at, but fellows, by their faces, of the strongest spirit. Come full speed to Bristol. John Trelawney."

I said goodbye to my mother and at last set off to Bristol. The doctor had gone the night before, and he and the squire were waiting for me at a large inn.

"Bravo! Here you are," cried the squire excitedly. "The ship's company is complete. We sail tomorrow! Come—you must meet Silver and Captain Smollett before we sail."

Now, to tell you the truth, from the first mention of Long John Silver, I had taken a fear in my mind that he might prove to be the very one-legged sailor whom I had watched for at the Admiral Benbow. But one look at this clean and pleasant-tempered man was enough for me to be convinced that he was no buccaneer, and I immediately warmed to the strange old fellow.

I even warmed to his parrot, who would sit on his shoulder and say repeatedly, "Pieces of eight! Pieces of eight!" Long John spoke of her fondly, making me think he was the very best of men.

The Captain, Mr. Smollett, was a different kettle of fish altogether. He was sharp-looking and seemed angry with everything and everyone on board. He was soon to tell me, Trelawney, and Livesey why.

"Well, sir," he addressed the squire. "Better to speak plain, I believe, even at the risk of offense. I don't like this cruise, and I don't like the men. That's the short and sweet."

The squire was angry to hear this, but the doctor asked Smollett to explain himself some more.

"I don't like that all the men on board seem to know more about the plans for this journey than I do, like the fact that I have only just found out that we are going after treasure. Too many people know about this treasure, and that's foolhardy." Captain Smollett sighed as he continued. "As for the men, I don't like them, sir. I think I should have had the choosing of my own hands."

"In other words, you fear a mutiny?" asked Dr. Livesey.

"I wouldn't say so in so many words, but it is the captain's job to be cautious," replied Captain Smollett. "I recommend that you keep all Silver's men together, in one cabin room, away from the area on the ship where we're keeping the arms and gunpowder ... just to be on the safe side."

And with that, he left to organize the crew so that we could set sail on the next tide.

I am not going to relate the voyage in detail, but before we arrived at Treasure Island, something happened that I must record. Captain Smollett had been right not to trust the crew chosen by Long John Silver.

On deck there was an apple barrel for anyone to help himself to fruit whenever he fancied. On the last night of our voyage, I had just climbed into this barrel to get an apple from the bottom when I heard some voices nearby.

"... I was Cap'n Flint's second-in-command, and I knows all about the treasure buried on this island," Silver was explaining to several of his men. "If you join me, we can all get a share of the riches. Then, as soon as we get the treasure on board, I'll finish with the Captain and his men on the island."

I was so shaken by Silver's words that I decided to stay hidden in the barrel. I realized with great fear that Silver was actually a pirate and that he was indeed planning a mutiny!

The men toasted each other with a drink of rum. "Here's to Captain Flint, and here's to us and plenty of prizes!"

Just then, as the moon rose in the night sky, the voice of the lookout shouted, "Land ahoy!"

In the following chaos, as the crew rushed on deck, I crept out of the barrel and ran to tell the Captain and the squire what I had overheard.

After listening carefully, the Captain thanked me, turned to the squire, and said, "We can't let on that we know of their plans. Otherwise, there'll be a mutiny right now. We have time until we find the treasure. I believe there are seven of us, including the boy and ourselves, whom we can rely on. So we must be prepared to fight these nineteen scoundrels."

The next day, with the *Hispaniola* safely anchored offshore, Captain Smollett gave orders for the men to go ashore for an afternoon off. Silver and twelve of his men eagerly got the boats ready. It was at this point that it occurred to me to slip ashore with the pirates to see what they were up to.

I hid in one of the boats and, as soon as it reached the beach, I swung myself out and plunged into the nearest thicket. Silver saw me and started shouting my name, but I paid him no attention. Jumping and ducking, I ran until I could run no more.

I began to enjoy myself and looked around me with some interest at the strange land that I was in. I had crossed a marshy area full of odd swampy trees, and now I had come out upon the outskirts of an open piece of undulating, sandy country. On the far side of this stood a hill with two craggy peaks shining vividly in the sun.

I had just reached a long thicket of oaklike trees when I heard Silver's voice. Trembling with fear, I dived for cover.

"I like you, Tom," Silver was saying. "That's why I'm asking you to join us, to save your neck."

"I'd rather lose my hand than join you scoundrels ..." Tom started to shout.

Just then, a terrible scream rose through the trees.

"What was that?" cried Tom.

"Oh, I reckon that'll be Alan," grinned Silver.

"God rest his soul," murmured Tom, realizing his friend must be dead. "As for you, John Silver, you're a mate of mine no more. Kill me, too, if you can."

And, with that, this brave fellow turned his back on Silver and set off walking for the beach. With a cry, Silver seized a branch and hurled it at the man. It hit him with stunning violence, right between the shoulders. Tom's hands flew up, he gave a sort of gasp, and he fell to the ground, dead.

I do not know what it rightly is to faint, but I do know that for the next little while the whole world swam away from before me in a whirling mist. Then, trembling, I crawled out of the thicket and ran, as fast as I could, away from the monster that was Long John Silver.

A while later, I stopped to get my bearings. It was then that I became aware of a strange figure darting among the trees ahead. What was this new danger?

Grasping my dagger, I gathered my courage and walked briskly toward the figure.

"Who are you?" I asked.

"I'm Ben Gunn," the strange man answered, his voice hoarse. His clothes were in tatters and his skin was darkened by the sun. "I was marooned three years ago. I was with Flint's crew when he buried the treasure. But he tricked me and left me stranded on the island. Please help me to escape!"

I felt sorry for Gunn, even though he had been part of Flint's pirate crew. I was starting to tell him my tale when we heard the distant boom of what sounded like a cannon being fired.

"They have begun to fight!" I cried. "Follow me—I must get back to help my friends." And we set off at a run, back toward the beach.

I found out later that Dr. Livesey, Mr. Trelawney, Captain Smollett, and the three faithful hands had battled with the six men that Silver had left on board the *Hispaniola*, and had managed to escape from the ship, taking some food supplies and arms to an old fort they had spied on shore. They had persuaded one of Silver's men, Abraham Gray, to switch sides and join them.

They were now holed up in the fort, and this was how I found them, preparing themselves for a long battle with Silver and his remaining men.

For my part, I was greatly relieved to find my friends, and they were glad to see me, as they had feared for my safety. I told them about my strange encounter with Ben Gunn, and his bizarre story.

Captain Smollett gave us all jobs and divided us into watches. We collected firewood and ate a hearty meal of pork.

Throughout the night, we took turns guarding our fort. As the sun rose on another day, we saw someone hobbling toward us. It was Long John Silver.

"Who goes there? Stand down or we fire!" shouted Captain Smollett.

"Flag of truce," cried Silver. "Cap'n Silver, sir, to come and make terms."

"I have no desire to talk to you. If you wish to talk to me, you can come forward. We won't shoot," replied Smollett.

"We're willing to submit, if we can come to terms," said Silver. "We want that treasure. You have a chart, haven't you?"

"That may be, but I'll never give it to you," cried Smollett.

Silver's face went bright red. "I'll attack your ol' fort before an hour's out. You'll be wishing you'd listened to ol' Long John Silver then!" With that, he stumbled off and disappeared among the trees.

True to his word, within the hour, Silver was back with his men. A terrible battle followed. As pirates swarmed over the fort's walls, swords clashed and screams pierced the air.

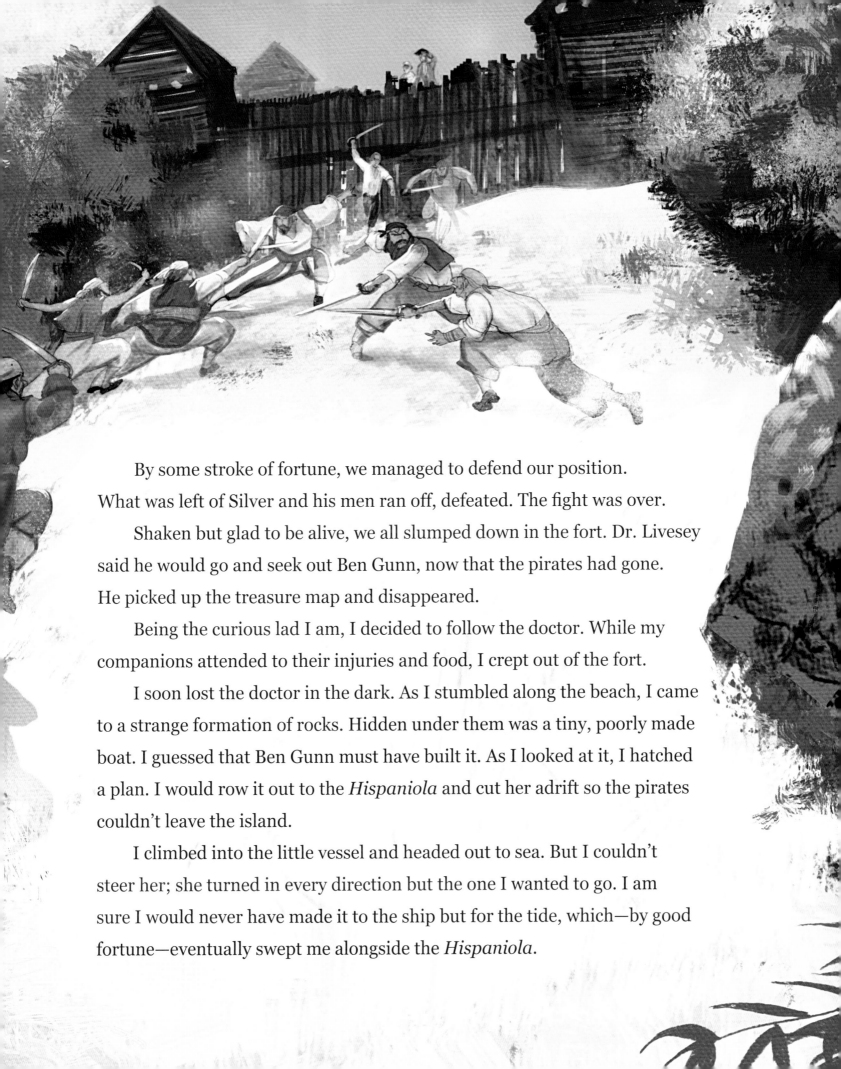

By some stroke of fortune, we managed to defend our position. What was left of Silver and his men ran off, defeated. The fight was over.

Shaken but glad to be alive, we all slumped down in the fort. Dr. Livesey said he would go and seek out Ben Gunn, now that the pirates had gone. He picked up the treasure map and disappeared.

Being the curious lad I am, I decided to follow the doctor. While my companions attended to their injuries and food, I crept out of the fort.

I soon lost the doctor in the dark. As I stumbled along the beach, I came to a strange formation of rocks. Hidden under them was a tiny, poorly made boat. I guessed that Ben Gunn must have built it. As I looked at it, I hatched a plan. I would row it out to the *Hispaniola* and cut her adrift so the pirates couldn't leave the island.

I climbed into the little vessel and headed out to sea. But I couldn't steer her; she turned in every direction but the one I wanted to go. I am sure I would never have made it to the ship but for the tide, which—by good fortune—eventually swept me alongside the *Hispaniola*.

I grabbed the anchor rope, hauled myself up, and clambered onto the deck. The ship was eerily quiet. I could see two pirates lying in a pool of blood. One was definitely dead. The other groaned and muttered, "Rum!"

It was Israel Hands, Silver's second-in-command.

Hands looked at me slyly. "What are you doing here, boy?"

"I've come to take possession of this ship, and you'll please regard me as your captain until further notice," I replied, faking more courage than I felt.

Hands grimaced at me. "I reckon, Cap'n Hawkins, you'll be wanting to get ashore now. S'pose we strike a deal. I can help you sail this ship back to the island."

It seemed to me that there was some sense in this plan, so we set sail. But as we neared the shoreline, Hands suddenly lunged at me. I clambered up the rigging to escape.

"Stand down!" I cried, as I pointed my dagger at him.

Hands roared and hurled his dagger at me. The blade knocked me on the shoulder. As I cried out, my dagger fell down onto Hands. He screamed and plunged head first into the sea.

Shaking, but fortunately not seriously injured, I secured the *Hispaniola*, dropped gently overboard, and swam to shore. I was eager to get back to my friends.

It was dark by the time I reached the fort. With a sigh of relief, I crept inside. Then a pair of hands grabbed me. I was surrounded by pirates!

"Hello, Jim," laughed Silver. "I've always liked you, lad. You've got spirit. As you can see, your friends are gone. You'll have to join up with ol' Cap'n Silver now. And I've got the treasure map!"

I gasped. How had he gotten the map? And what had happened to my friends?

The next day, Silver announced that the pirates were going treasure hunting and that he was taking me with them so I couldn't escape. Flint's map said his treasure was buried under a tall tree below a hill.

As we neared the place marked with a red cross on the map, one of the men ahead started shouting. The other pirates ran toward him. At the foot of a big pine tree lay a human skeleton.

We were staring at this gruesome sight when, all of a sudden, out of the trees in front of us, a high, trembling voice struck up with the words, "Fifteen men on the dead man's chest, yo-ho-ho, and a bottle of rum!"

I have never seen men more dreadfully affected than the pirates. "It's the ghost of Cap'n Flint!" cried one of the men.

Silver managed to gather his courage. "Lads, it's someone trying to scare us. Come, let's find this treasure."

Up ahead was another tall tree. "That's the spot, lads!" cried Silver. But as we approached the tree, we could see a great big hole in the ground below it. Silver let out a low groan. Flint's treasure had been found by someone else!

"You dragged us all this way, and for what?" one of the pirates roared as he pointed his dagger at Silver.

But, just then, cries rang out from the nearby thicket, and Dr. Livesey and Ben Gunn came rushing out of the trees. The terrified pirates ran off.

Silver, however, stayed where he was. "Thank you kindly, doctor," he laughed. "You came in the nick of time for me and Jim! If you'll take me from this cursed island, I'll cause you no further troubles!"

The doctor nodded his agreement, quietly planning to turn Silver over to the authorities once we got back to Bristol.

As we set off toward the rest of the group, Dr. Livesey filled us in on what had happened. Ben Gunn, it seemed, had found the treasure several years before, dug it up, and hidden it in a cave.

I was very relieved to see all my friends again, and even happier when, a few days later, after having transported all the treasure to the *Hispaniola*, we lifted the anchor and left that ill-fated island behind.

Trelawney, sharing the doctor's plans for Silver, allowed the old pirate to travel home with us. However, Silver, being the crafty man he was, managed to sneak ashore and disappear with some of the gold at one of the ports we stopped at on the way home.

As for the rest of us, we returned home, each with a large share of the treasure, which we used wisely or foolishly, according to our natures. I never returned to that accursed island. I sometimes think of it, though, remembering the pained look on Long John Silver's face, the moment he realized the treasure was gone and his pirate dreams of vast riches were shattered forever.